Chuck and Duck

Level 2B

Written by Sam Hay
Illustrated by Ann Johns

Ticktock

What is synthetic phonics?

Synthetic phonics teaches children to recognise the sounds of letters and to blend 'synthesise' them together to make whole words.

Understanding sound/letter relationships gives children the confidence and ability to read unfamiliar words, without having to rely on memory or guesswork; this helps them progress towards independent reading.

Did you know? Spoken English uses more than 40 speech sounds. Each sound is called a *phoneme*. Some phonemes relate to a single letter (d-o-g) and others to combinations of letters (sh-ar-p). When a phoneme is written down it is called a *grapheme*. Teaching these sounds, matching them to their written form and sounding out words for reading is the basis of synthetic phonics.

Consultant

I love reading phonics has been created in consultation
with language expert Abigail Steel. She has a
background in teaching and teacher training and is
a respected expert in the field of Synthetic Phonics.
Abigail Steel is a regular contributor to educational
publications. Her international education consultancy
supports parents and teachers in the promotion of
literacy skills.

Reading tips

This book focuses on the ch sound as in chip.

Tricky words in this book

Any words in bold may have unusual spellings or are new and have not yet been introduced.

> ### Tricky words in this book:
>
> ## said   to   for   ball
> ## was   I   my   the

Extra ways to have fun with this book

After the reader has finished the story, ask them questions about what they have just read:

What is Duck good at?
Why did Fred go red?

Explain that the two letters 'ch' make one sound. Think of other words that use the 'ch' sound, such as *chip* and *chat*.

I like to read and quack. My favourite place to read is in the park. Quack!

A pronunciation guide

This grid highlights the sounds used in the story and offers a guide on how to say them.

s as in sat	a as in ant	t as in tin	p as in pig	i as in ink
n as in net	c as in cat	e as in egg	h as in hen	r as in rat
m as in mug	d as in dog	g as in get	o as in ox	u as in up
l as in log	f as in fan	b as in bag	j as in jug	v as in van
w as in wet	z as in zip	y as in yet	k as in kit	qu as in quick
x as in box	ff as in off	ll as in ball	ss as in kiss	zz as in buzz
ck as in duck	pp as in puppy	nn as in bunny	rr as in arrow	gg as in egg
dd as in daddy	bb as in chubby	tt as in attic	sh as in shop	ch as in chip
th as in them				

Be careful not to add an 'uh' sound to 's', 't', 'p', 'c', 'h', 'r', 'm', 'd', 'g', 'l', 'f' and 'b'. For example, say 'fff' not 'fuh' and 'sss' not 'suh'.

Chuck got a shock.
A duck sat on his mat.

'Yes?' **said** Chuck.
'Quack!' said Duck.

Chuck went **to** chop a log.
Duck went as well.

Chuck went **for** a jog.
Duck went as well!

Chuck met his chum Fred,
and his pet dog Chip.

Chuck and Fred had a chat.

'Duck is a dull pet,' said Fred.

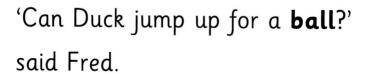

'Can Duck jump up for a **ball**?'
said Fred.

'Not much,' said Chuck.

'Can Duck run fast?' said Fred.

'Not as such,' said Chuck.

'Duck is such a dull pet,' said Fred.

Duck went off in a huff.

But Fred and Chuck got a shock.

Duck **was** back.
Duck had set up chess!

A rich man went past.
'**I** wish Duck was **my** pet.
How much?' said **the** man.

'Bad luck,' said Chuck.
'Duck is my pet and best chum.'
Fred went red!

OVER **48** TITLES IN SIX LEVELS
Abigail Steel recommends...

Some titles from Level 1

Bad Rat
978-1-84898-600-8

The Best Gift
978-1-84898-603-9

Clint and Grant Play I-Spy
978-1-78325-098-1

Gran and Bret's Trip
978-1-78325-100-1

Other titles to enjoy from Level 2

Wish Fish
978-1-84898-604-6

Let's go to the Swings
978-1-78325-102-5

Kyle in Trouble
978-1-78325-101-8

Some titles from Level 3

Bart's Go-Cart
978-1-78325-105-6

Queen Ella's Feet
978-1-84898-609-1

Puff Flies
978-1-84898-610-7

The Pop Duet
978-1-78325-108-7

An Hachette UK Company
www.hachette.co.uk

Copyright © Octopus Publishing Group Ltd 2012
First published in Great Britain in 2012 by TickTock, an imprint of Octopus Publishing Group Ltd,
Endeavour House, 189 Shaftesbury Avenue, London WC2H 8JY.
www.octopusbooks.co.uk
www.ticktockbooks.co.uk

ISBN 978 1 84898 605 3

Printed and bound in China
10 9 8 7 6 5 4 3